The Dragon Bone Journal

2025 ISSUE

Copyright Page

TRIGGER WARNINGS:

Death, Religious Trauma, Cults

Upcoming Releases

I Love You Unconventionally
An Anthology on the Expanse of Love
Compiled by Effie Joe Stock
& Nathaniel Luscombe

Love spans farther than the most distant star and deeper than the darkest ocean.

With three main categories: Familial, Platonic, and Romantic, the expanse of all types of love are explored in this collection of short stories and poetry. From loving your spouse if they turned into a worm, to fantastical dangers faced by a mother desperately learning how to love her child, to cherishing friendships in a world dominated by romance, and even never giving up on a sister drawn by sirens, I Love You Unconventionally is an anthology like no other. Filled with the strangest and most relatable types of love, this anthology will leave you with a warm heart and a different understanding of what love truly means.

Human Scars on Planet Skin
by Nathaniel Luscombe
& Effie Joe Stock

Turr is fighting back for what was stolen from her: her body and her children living on it. After the humans tried to colonize her, Turr was forced to resort to mass violence to reclaim her skin. But in fleeing the planet of Turr, the humans left behind a chemical disaster—the dead zone. To bring peace and life back to herself, Turr sends out a desperate plea to two shroom people: Invidia and Clyra. Invidia, though surrounded by death, is tasked with learning how to breathe life back into the land. Clyra must lead a group of broken failed experiments through the forest, following a trail of visions. Death and uncertainty face them at every turn, but only when they're all together can the planet truly begin to heal.

A science-fantasy like nothing you've ever read before, Human Scars on Planet Skin will leave you haunted by the stark realities of upsetting the balance of life, aching against the sorrow unmitigated death brings, and shivering against the horror of being trapped inside your own body. But more than anything, this novella will leave you comforted, knowing hope always exists in the life around us, no matter how dark our surroundings.

Dragon Heart Press

An All New Poetry Imprint

There is no better way to peer into the soul than by reading and writing poetry. On a quest to lend voice to the deepest, most raw sectors of the human experience, Dragon Bone Publishing is expanding with an all-new poetry imprint,

DRAGON HEART PRESS.

Dragon Bone Publishing is excited to announce our expansion with a new imprint—Dragon Heart Press! Dragon Heart Press (DHP) will be home to DBP's upcoming poetry projects. Heading this imprint are Nathaniel Luscombe and MJ Anthony, who are both beyond excited to curate a collection of poetry bursting with heart, warmth, and truth. The label will debut in 2025 with four exceptional releases.

Follow them on:
Instagram @dragon.heart.press
or
www.dragonbonepublishing.com/dragonheartpress
for more news!

Nathaniel Luscombe

All of Us Parallel

time is but an orchestra
past present future
the three tender strings
that cut through a universe
beyond our comprehension

no fingers could coax them
to make a sound so sweet
it would break our pain

we are all of us parallel
playing out our roles
in a never ending cycle
birthing bleeding dying
again and again and again

Nathaniel Luscombe is an up-and-coming author from Ontario, Canada. He is best known for Moon Soul and The Planets We Become, and has also been in a handful of anthologies. He fills his time with a full-time job, lots of book ideas, and the responsibilities that come with co-running Dragon Bone Publishing.

M.J. Anthony

On Enviornmental Stressors

if i could mold one week from clay
i'd call it peace, and let us rest,
decree smallness and security; tell
heart and flesh they've done their best

the mourning clouds will call in truant;
sunlight gild our cracks in gold
dewy grass will brush our self-hood's legs
(i swear, the night will not stay cold)

at the waist, we'll cup our organs,
at the ribcage, brush the heart,
hug touch-starved bones back into places
so that we do not fall apart.

M.J. Anthony has been writing since they could first hold a crayon. At present, they are a poet and speculative fiction writer living in the Greater Boston area, a community librarian, and the author of several short stories as well as a 2025 poetry collection with Dragon Heart Press. Their current life is the manifestation of a dream for them, and they count themself incredibly blessed to be surrounded by the friends, loved ones, and very special cats who have made it all possible.

2025 Dragon Heart Press Debut Releases

WHEN ONE WORLD ENDS, ANOTHER BEGINS
A POETRY COLLECTION
BY NATHANIEL LUSCOMBE

Words became my bloodletting. I've been bleeding now for years.

At times playful, at times heartbreaking, *When One World Ends, Another Begins* is a raw, honest window into what it looks like to live. Nathaniel explores the cyclical nature of existence, touching on themes of mental health, body image, faith and fear. Above all, he examines what it means to be human, peeling back all the ugly layers to find the beauty within.

ON THE CARE AND FEEDING OF DREAMERS
BY MJ ANTHONY

Today I am learning to take anxiety by the hand and teach this trembling, fragile beast that we are (and yet will be) okay.

In their debut collection, MJ Anthony navigates a complicated web of intersecting topics such as complex trauma, neurodiversity, lasting illness, and practicing self-love in a body long-alienated from you. Alongside the reader, the author combs tangles into threads and weaves them into a gentler future, re-unifying selves and stories both old and new. Part hurting, part healing, and wholly original, The Care and Feeding of Dreamers is a love letter to everyone living with a broken body or a troubled mind.

THE LAST SCENT OF PINE
BY TYLER J. WELCH

www.tylerjwelch.com

When Tyler J. Welch isn't secluded in his Wisconsin dwelling, he can be found deeply engrossed within captivating forests and fog-smothered marshlands—embracing the depth of the world. It's in these secluded corners where he has found inspiration, developing ways to imbue his writing and photography with a distinctive dark artistic style. His work is unique and enticing, pulling us all to find the haunting secrets hidden within.

He lives with his loving wife and two sons, despises stark cold winters, and is in constant search for immortality. His debut novel End Realm releases fall 2024.

Pale worms dot the shallow lake. Lifeless they are, floating—most of their numbers that is. A nearby leopard frog takes its time paddling the lake through the massacre, in search for worms-not-so-pale, the living kind . . . the ones worth eating—digesting—to prolong its newly suffering life.

The paddling frog has an on-looker, a thinned out gray squirrel halfway up a red pine and starving. Its arms, legs, bushy tail hanging over the sides of this particular sodden and drowning king—like every other red pine ruler in this shallow death lake.

Squirrel's eyes watch Frog float more than swim through the clear poison below, but his little brain is elsewhere . . . Busy thinking of the properly good times. The times when nuts, shrooms, and more nuts were in such abundance that his thousands of cousins acted like goblins—adolescent, childish goblins—stealing and thieving from each other's hoards. Full well knowing it would aggravate them into frenzy . . . but nothing more. As there was so much food then . . . nuts, shrooms, and more nuts, that the stealing was just a fun game of jest. A pastime. And not one that would render the coming winter one of hunger.

His little brain is busy thinking of the times years ago when rains ended with grand grows, not grand flows. The times when the woodland floor was covered up to his chin with densely fallen red pine needles, not water surpassing the tips of his acute ears and twitching nose hairs.

Squirrel's eyes drift, but he shakes himself alive—his eyes drawing back down at Frog.

His little brain is far past wishing for food, it's been far too many days without and his little brain has given that notion up. He is now just hoping Sir Frog makes it. He is just hoping some of his cousins make it . . . He takes a labored but deep breath—his last one—and the rich red citrus scent of pine stings inside his nose, he is just now hoping the almighty trees make it.

Squirrel's eyes drift, his thin corpse rolls quietly off the red pine limb . . . and a cold somber splash echoes over the lake of death.

Katie Fitzgerald writes short stories in a variety of genres, from humor, to mystery, to contemporary, to kissing-only romance. A former librarian married to a librarian, she is a voracious reader and listener of audiobooks, and the careful curator of a large home library of children's books. She loves bookish tee shirts, Flannery O'Connor, song lyric jokes, and Little Free Libraries. Katie grew up in a small town in New York's Hudson Valley, but now lives in the Maryland suburbs with her husband and five kids.

THE TURN
OF THE TIDE
BY KATIE FITZGERALD

Kent was restocking the soda coolers at the back of Convenience Mart on Saturday night when Lucy stepped through the front door in a long green gown, dripping from head to toe. He was still smarting from what she'd said to him last week. What did she mean, she had to see how things went with Brian before she could make any commitments? He stifled a smirk. It seemed that karma had moved swiftly, at least.

Getting to his feet and wiping his hands on his khakis, Kent moved toward the register. Gesturing toward the rack of assorted umbrellas, he said, "If you're looking for one of those, I think it might be too late."

Lucy raised her eyebrows menacingly, then twisted the hem of her dress, squeezing out the excess water. Silently, Kent grabbed the WET FLOOR sign from the back room and placed it over the puddle she'd made. Then he leaned back casually against the check-out counter, stroking his beard and studying Lucy.

"Don't look at me like that," she snapped.

Kent put up his hands in surrender. "I'm not doing anything. It's hard to act normal when you look like you went six rounds with a dolphin. I knew the benefit dance had an Under the Sea theme, but surely they didn't mean – "

"Stop!" Lucy shouted. "You got what you wanted, so you can just stop!"

What he wanted? He wanted to be in the parish hall over at St. Bart's church, all dressed up like a million bucks, gliding Lucy around the room amidst paper decorations cut to look like seaweed. Nothing about this remotely resembled that.

"More accurately," Kent pointed out, "Brian got what I wanted." He made a big show of looking around for him. "Where is Prince Charming anyway?"

A flicker of anger moved across Lucy's face. "Obviously he's not here," she said.

"Waiting in the car?" Kent ventured.

Lucy shook her head. "I don't know where he is," she admitted softly. "He left me there with no ride home."

"In the rain?"

She nodded, sniffling.

"Well, that settles it." Kent stood up straight, then reached over to turn the sign on the door from OPEN to CLOSED.

"What are you doing?" Lucy's eyes widened. "You're not going to look for him! I'm humiliated enough."

Kent shook his head. "He's not worth it," he said. "But someone needs to look after you."

"You can't just close early because I had a bad night."

"Actually, since I'm the boss, that's exactly what I can do. Besides I can't have you saying you came to me in your hour of need and I hung you out to dry." Kent paused to let the joke sink in. His whole body relaxed when he saw Lucy give a small smile.

"Come on. I'll close up. Drive you home. We can watch The Little Mermaid. Or maybe Titanic."

Lucy vehemently shook her head.

"No? What then? Aquaman? Moby Dick? Jaws? Jaws could be good. We can imagine Brian as a little shark snack."

"Kent." Her facial expression matched her warning tone. "I think I prefer your dry sense of humor." Kent could hear the affection behind her every word and he felt warm all over.

Putting his arm around Lucy, Kent pulled her in close to his side. An imprint of moisture slowly formed against the fabric of his polo shirt, but he didn't care. Lucy leaned in closer and rested her head on Kent's shoulder. There was a moment's silence, then she spoke. "I made a mistake."

"Yup," Kent said matter-of-factly. "Going out with that guy was a big mistake."

"Not that," Lucy said. "I'm talking about what I said to you."

"You don't like the beard after all?" He feigned offense.

Lucy smacked him gently on the chest. "The other thing I said to you."

"The part about not being my girlfriend?"

"That, yes."

"Well, it's not like the offer expired or something. Even halfway drowned, you're still the most appealing woman I know." Kent bent down and kissed Lucy's forehead. After a moment, Lucy turned to face him and he captured her lips with his own.

"So," he said when the kiss broke. "Can we get out of here now? You're dripping all over my floor."

"Surely you're not going to let me drip all over your truck?"

"I have a tarp I can put down."

"Ah, such romance."

"That's nothing," he said. "Just you wait."

Kent hit the lights and locked the door, then intertwined his fingers with Lucy's. All the way to her place, he thought about how nice it was to test the waters, how good it felt to know that he was already in too deep.

BONFIRE BUDDIES
BY RHYKER DYE

Rhyker, a queer writer and Arkansas native, began writing as an academic. Building on skills honed as a non-fiction editor and researcher, he found a love for fiction writing. Most Saturdays, Rhyker can be found haunting the local coffee shops as he writes best alongside indie albums and whispered gossip.

```
{

        "Format_version":"1.17",

        "Xavier Episodic Memory:npc_dialogue":{

                "Scenes":[

                {

                        "Scene_tag":"asking_conner_out",

                        "Scene_location":"ENGL_2023_Classroom.zip",

                        "Npc_name":"Conner",

                        "On_open_command":"[

                                "/approach target @Conner",]

                { Input: Conner smiles.

                        [Outputs:

                                "Option 1":" "Hey, Conner.",

                                "Option 2":" "Command":"Run smile.exe",

                                "Option 3":" "Command":"Delete all dialogue.exe files",]

                }

                { Auto Select: Option 3

                        ["Command":"Delete all dialogue.exe files"]

            }

        ]

    }

                {Input: "Hey, Xavier."

                        [Outputs:

                                "Option 1":" ERROR. Missing data file,

                                "Option 2":" ERROR. Missing data file,

                                "Option 3":" ERROR. Missing data file,
```

}

]

}

{ERROR detected,

["error type":"missing data files,

"Command":" system reboot,

"Command":" recover dialogue.exe files,

"Command":" rerun interaction,]

}

]

}

{Input: "Hey, Xavier"

[Outputs:

"Option 1":" "Hey, are you going to the bonfire tonight?",

"Option 2":" "Hey.",

"Option 3":" "Hey. You should come to the bonfire with me tonight.",]

}

{Player select: Option 1

["Hey, are you going to the bonfire tonight?"]

}

]

}

{Input: "Yeah, Macey and I were planning on going together around 10:00."}

}

]

}

{ERROR detected,

["error type":"invalid input,

"Command":" system reboot,

"Command":" generate new dialogue.exe files,

"Command":" rerun interaction,]

                }

            ]

        }

{Input: "Yeah, Macey and I were planning on going together around 10:00."

    [Outputs:

        "Option 1":" "Don't go with Macey. Go with me.",

        "Option 2":" "I thought you were gay.",

        "Option 3":" "Going together?",]

    }

{Player select: Option 3

    ["Going together?"]

        }

            ]

        }

{Input: "Macey's volunteer shift for her sorority ends then so that's when I'm

    showing up. I don't want to lurk around killing time until she's free."

    [Outputs:

        "Option 1":" "You wouldn't have to lurk if I went with you.",

        "Option 2":" "If you want to show up earlier, I could go with you.",

        "Option 3":" "I can think of a few ways we could kill time.",]

    }

{Player select: Option 2

    ["If you want to show up earlier, I could go with you.",]

        }

            ]

        }

{Input: "I thought you hated crowds. I wouldn't want you to be uncomfortable."

    [Outputs:

        "Option 1":" "I'm never uncomfortable when I'm with you.",

        "Option 2":" "I'm trying to get out more.",

        "Option 3":" "Why does everyone think I'm antisocial?!",]

}
{Auto select: Option 3

["Why does everyone think I'm antisocial?!",

"Command":" Run "stop_being_defensive.patch",

"Command":" Rerun player selection,]
{Player Select: Option 2

["I'm trying to get out more."]

}

]

}

{Input: "Oh, that's cool. I could use some more friends."

}

]

}

{ERROR detected,

["error type":" friendzoned,

"Command":" system reboot,

"Command":" generate new dialogue.exe files,

"Command":" rerun interaction,

}

]

}

{Input: "Oh, that's cool. I could use some more friends."

[Outputs:

"Option 1":" "Are we friends?",

"Option 2":" "Happy to help.",

"Option 3":" "I'm not trying to be friends with you, Conner.",]

}
{Player select: Option 1

["Are we friends?"]

}

]

    }

            {Input: "Definitely. Would you want to meet there around 8:30? Do you want to stay to

            hang out with Macey when she's free?"

                    [Outputs:

                            "Option 1":" "Sure, whatever sounds best to you.",

                            "Option 2":" "I'd rather not hang out with Macey.",

                            "Option 3":" "Sure, but I wouldn't want to third wheel since you and

                                    Macey already have plans.",]

                    }

            {Player select: Option 3

                    ["Sure, but I wouldn't want to third wheel since you and Macey already have

                            plans.",]

            }

        ]

    }

            {Input: "Wouldn't Macey be the third wheel if we're the one's on the date?"

        }

        }

    }

            {ERROR detected,

                    ["error type":" invalid response,

                            "Command":" system reboot,

                            "Command":" generate new dialogue.exe files,

                            "Command":" rerun interaction,]

            }

        ]

    }

            {Input: "Wouldn't Macey be the third wheel if we're the one's on the date?"

                    [Outputs:

                            "Option 1":" "Who said it was a date?",

"Option 2":" "Is it a date? I thought you just wanted to be bonfire

buddies.",

"Option 3":" "Oh, thank God. It is a date then.",]

}

{Player select: Option 2

["Is it a date? I thought you just wanted to be bonfire buddies..",]

}

]

}

{Input: Bonfire buddies? That sounds like something frat boys tell each other before they make out. 'No homo, man. We're just bonfire buddies.'"

}

]

}

{ERROR detected,

["error type":" incorrect player selection,

"Command":" run cringe.exe,

"Command":" run search query":"nearest bridge to jump off",

"Command":" run spiraling.exe,]

}

]

}

{Input: Conner laughs.

["Command":" cancel search query,

"Command":" system reboot,]

}

}

}

{Input: "Here, give me your phone."

[Outputs:

"Option 1":" "Why?",

"Option 2":" "command":"hand Conner the phone",

"Option 3":" "command":"cringe out of existence",]

}

{Player select: Option 2

["command":"hand Conner the phone",]

}

]

}

{Input: Conner types.

[Outputs:

"Option 1":" "Command":"stand awkwardly",

"Option 2":" "What are you doing?",

"Option 3":" "Command":"panic+grab the phone back",]

}

{Player select: Option 1

["Command":"stand awkwardly",]

}

]

}

{Input: Conner gives back the phone. "I'll see you tonight."

[Outputs:

"Option 1":" "Can't wait!",

"Option 2":" "Not if I see you first",

"Option 3":" "Command":"panic+forget to reply+look at the phone",]

}

{Player select: Option 3

["Command":"panic+forget to reply+look at the phone",]

}

]

}

{Input: Contact Added. "Bonfire Buddy<3"

                }

        ]

    }

        {ERROR detected,

            ["error type":" invalid input,

                "Command":" run butterflies.exe,

                "Command":" run blush.exe,

                "Command":" run system reboot,]

        }

    ]

}

        {"Command":" Archive memory.}

Ashley Schaller is an award-winning author who prefers tea over coffee and proudly wears the title of "Dog Mom". As a writer, she seeks to create stories that glorify God. Stories that entertain, but you never have to worry about the content.

Instagram: @ashleyschallerauthor

THE MUSIC BOX
BY ASHLEY SCHALLER

The girl danced, unable to stop.

Turning, turning, turning.

Always turning.

Yet never growing dizzy. Tutu sparkling, pristine as ever. Shoes never wearing out. Beautiful as the day she'd first begun.

Cogs whirred, mechanical and precise. No step ever out of place.

This was her curse.

Her gift.

She'd wished to be beautiful and now she was. Stunning. Something to be looked at, but rarely touched.

Porcelain legs locked in place, the best dancer in the land. Music so poetic, wrapped her in its spell. Addicting, yet loathsome to her ear.

Twirling on her music box, for all eternity.

Live and Learn

Helpful Articles by Amatuer and Professional Writers

FOR GRANDPA
BY HALEY THOMPSON

Aisling Revell knew at thirteen that she would never love anything as much as telling stories. She has had work published in her college's literary journal, and hopes to publish the novels she's working on in the future. When she isn't writing she loves to read, spend time outdoors, and snuggle with her cat, Gracie.

I was never close with my grandfather.

A sad fact to admit, but true nonetheless. Although I saw him on holidays when I was younger, family gatherings became challenging after my parents' divorce, so it was rare to see him even once a year as I got older. At the age of seventeen, I barely knew him, and he barely knew me. And yet there I was, walking into a hospital to see him before he died.

I've always hated hospitals. I know that's not an unpopular opinion. Afterall, the sight of blood makes some people queasy, and who isn't scared of needles from time to time? To top it all off, hospitals are oftentimes associated with death. These were never my reasons though. Sure, death freaked me as much as the next person, but something else put me at unease. Hospitals just have an air of awkwardness. People never seem to know how to act when they are visiting them and the blinding white walls make one forget the time of day.

This hospital did a decent enough job at covering up the awkward atmosphere, with floral paintings that reminded me of Grandma's house, but the dimly lit lobby and the unattended reception desk were unnerving.

Mom was carelessly chatting and joking about how terrible at directions she was and how long it would take us to find the right room. Humor was her way of dealing with difficult situations. Humor was her way of dealing with everything. I laughed along with her, commenting that I wasn't the best person to bring along since I inherited her sense of direction. Maybe humor was my way of dealing with difficult situations too.

The hallways were eerily quiet except for the occasional cough from someone. I tried my hardest to not glance at patients as we walked past their rooms, but my curiosity always won in the end. Many of them were old. Some of them had family visiting. All of them made me want to avert my gaze. For a moment I wondered how many of them were dying, but I shook this morbid thought away.

We somehow managed to find our way to the elevator and the ICU, taking many wrong turns before we got there. Mom said nothing as we entered the room we were looking for. She took a seat next to the sleeping patient in bed. Her dad. My grandpa.

I sat down in the empty seat next to my grandpa's wife, smiling at her as I did so.

The room was a decent size, but cramped with all of the equipment and chairs for visitors. A beeping noise came from one of the many machines, but I didn't care enough to determine which one. A bouquet made up of every color in the rainbow sat on a table in the corner. It looked rather tacky if I'm being honest, but I suppose the sentiment was sweet.

Mom rubbed Grandpa's hand softly, tears forming in her eyes. Feeling out of place, I looked down at the notebook on my lap. I brought it with me to work on story ideas for my creative writing class, and considered leaving it in the car, worried everyone would see it as rude, but it would be a welcome distraction. I didn't want to see my mom cry. I didn't want to see a man hooked up to machines with a breathing mask over his face, looking small and weak in that big bed.

I wish I could say that I was there for the right reasons. I wish I could say I was there because he was my grandpa and this might have been the last time I got to see him, but that's just not true. When he died, nothing about my life would change.

I barely knew him. He barely knew me.

The only reason I came was Mom. This whole ordeal had taken a toll on her, and she could use the support, even if she wouldn't explicitly ask for it. Instead, she would make comments about how she wasn't looking forward to the drive until one of the kids volunteered to go with her. This time it was me.

Grandpa quit smoking long before the cancer was detected, but it didn't make a difference because what started in his lungs spread through his entire body. Mom was already warned that he likely wouldn't be coming out of the hospital alive, but this also wasn't the first time she'd been told this. A roller coaster of emotions for everyone involved, and I wasn't sure how much more of it Mom could take.

I sank further into my chair and gripped my notebook tightly, wanting nothing more than to just disappear into the walls.

In the afternoon, Grandpa woke up and was doing well, considering his condition. He found enough energy to sit up, revealing the mole on his left shoulder blade through the open back of the hospital gown. All of the machines and tubes were probably annoying him, but he never complained. He was polite to the nurses, which explained why many of them took a liking to him, and he even managed some jokes. Mom mentioned he was always an easy going guy.

I remained silent most of the time, waiting for the arrival of my uncle. He lived out of state so I rarely got to see him, and while the reason for his coming was unfortunate, his visits were always welcome. He would no doubt be able to lift everyone's spirits with his outgoing personality, even if his "pull my finger" pranks did get old.

"Haley, what do you plan on doing after school?"

The question from my grandpa's wife pulled me out of my thoughts. As a senior, this was a question that I was used to hearing, and it never failed to annoy me. Everyone forgot what it was like to be a teenager with your entire life ahead of you, scared and unsure of what the future would bring. Questions like that only made the anxiety worse. Everyone was just "trying to help", so if you said any of this you were being ungrateful. I resisted the urge to roll my eyes and instead opened my mouth to give the same generic answer that I gave everybody.

"She's going to write a book."

My head snapped in the direction of Grandpa, not believing my ears. His words may have been muffled because of the mask, but that was what he said.

How did he know about that? That was what I wanted, but...

I was ready to give her the generic answer. Tell her that I planned on going to community college first to figure out what I wanted to do, before transferring somewhere else. After all, everyone always nodded when I said this, saying it was the "smart" thing to do. Save some money, and decide what's best for me, but Grandpa took the words right out of my mind. He gave the answer that I always wanted to give, but never did because of how others reacted to it. Because of the odd smirks and raised eyebrows. Because they always asked about my backup plan. Because they clearly saw it as nothing more than an idealistic dream. The worst part was I was starting to believe it too.

Sure, writing was what I wanted to do, but what were the odds of that happening? Being a best-selling author is the dream of so many others. So many others who were probably more talented than I could ever hope to be. What made me so special? Thinking it could actually be a possibility felt conceited. Even though I knew at thirteen that there would never be anything in this world I loved doing more than telling stories, I always assumed I would have to settle in life. Grandpa, on the other hand, seemed to think otherwise.

I ran my hand over the cover of my notebook, smiling. Maybe my grandpa did know me.

I twirled my pen in my fingers, willing myself to think of story ideas, but coming up short.

Mom and I were in the waiting area just down the hall, giving my uncle some alone time with Grandpa. I glanced around, taking in the simple features of the room. It was adequate, with a few sofas and a small television. A large painting on the wall depicted an autumn day, the bright hues of the trees reflected in a bright blue pond. My eyes landed on Mom. She was rather upset about the lack of up-to-date magazines to steal. The ones the hospital did have were unworthy of taking up space in her purse.

This was the perfect time to resume brainstorming ideas for a story, but my thoughts kept returning to what Grandpa said.

"She's going to write a book."

With those six, simple words, Grandpa seemed to understand what I wanted more than anyone did. More than I did. He didn't say it sarcastically or try to sugarcoat it, he just said it. Plain and simple. No ifs, ands, or buts about it.

He had the courage to say what I couldn't.

"Mom, did you tell Grandpa that I wanted to be a writer?"

"I brought it up once a while ago that you liked writing, but I'm surprised he remembered."

He remembered. He remembered something about the granddaughter he barely knew. His ungrateful granddaughter who didn't even want to be there.

He knew something about me that people I talked to everyday didn't know, and he said it with conviction, without an odd smirk or a raised eyebrow. Like it was a no-brainer. Like he had no doubt in his mind that I would do it.

"You know you have to do it now," Mom said.

"I know. I will."

During the next few days, Grandpa's condition was beginning to give everyone whiplash. One minute he was alert and laughing, asking for a beer, and the next he was mistaking Mom for a nurse. Mom and I could never guess how we would find him when we drove up to visit.

Sadly, the doctors were right this time. Grandpa wasn't going to be coming out of the hospital alive.

I never thought I'd visit him more than once while he was in the hospital. I never thought I'd end up missing two tests because I chose to sleep on the uncomfortable waiting room couch on a school night. I never thought I would spend hours at a hospital because I wanted to, and not because I felt like I had to. I never thought I'd find myself regretting not having had more of a relationship with him, after seeing what a kind, gentle man he was in his final days. I never thought I'd be present in the room when he died.

I stood just inside the doorway as a few nurses rushed in to check his pulse, confirming that he was gone. Late at night, the hospital was even quieter than it had been during the day. My aunt asked if I was okay. Mom hugged me. A few minutes later, everyone gathered in the hallway right outside of the room, telling stories about Grandpa as if he had died a long time ago instead of moments prior. They were all crying and smiling at the same time. Sad that he was gone, relieved that his suffering was finally over.

I took a moment to look at Grandpa one more time, before turning away, hot tears falling down my cheeks.

"Just you wait, Grandpa. I'm going to write that book. I promise."

Mom takes solace in the fact that Grandpa opened his eyes one last time and looked at her right before he died. As if that was his way of saying goodbye. Dad claims that Grandpa was so high on pain medication that he probably couldn't see her.

I've told other people about what Grandpa told me. Some seem just as touched as me, while others just nod and smile, even though it's evident that they don't understand its importance.

I'm not even sure why it was so important. Why those words meant so much to me. I barely knew him, and he barely knew me, but for some reason, that made it more significant. Grandpa never read any of my work, and unfortunately, he never will. I have no idea what he would have thought of it. Maybe he would have loved it, maybe he would have hated it. Maybe he was so high on pain medication he didn't realize what he was saying.

The sensible part of me acknowledges that Grandpa probably didn't know what he was doing when he said those words to me. That he would end up inspiring me to the point that I promised I would dedicate my first book to him.

None of that mattered. Whether he meant them or not, those words made me acknowledge something important. If I viewed my writing the way everyone else did, as just a fanciful hobby that would lead nowhere, that's all it would ever be. I had to stop saying if, and start saying when.

In the years following my grandfather's death, my mom has commented numerous times that the mole on my left shoulder blade is identical to the one he had. It fills me with a strange sense of pride knowing that I have that connection with him, and I always silently thank him for what he has given me.

Even in my twenties, I still give vague answers about my future at times. There are still unknowns about where my life is headed, but I never say that I'm trying to figure out what I want to do, because I know what I want to do. I want to write.

The amused expressions don't bother me much anymore. If anything, they drive me to achieve my goal. Although I want to prove them wrong, what I want most of all is to prove Grandpa right. When my time comes, I want to be able to face him and say,

"Grandpa, I wrote that book."

Nathaniel Luscombe is an author from Ontario, Canada. When not reading or writing, you can find him thinking about reading and writing. He writes across many genres, has been published in multiple anthologies, and is busy working on more sci-fi and science fantasy works.

THE IMPORTANCE OF VARIETY IN SCIENCE FICTION
BY NATHANIEL LUSCOMBE

Instagram: @nathaniel.luscombe

Science fiction has always been more than just a genre. Some might say it's a vision, a narrow scope into humanity's potential future. It's a combination of ideas, dreams, hopes, and fears that fuel a fictional future for humanity. It makes sense that as technology develops, it often mirrors fictional technology used in sci-fi. As writers come up with ideas, there are scientists working to make these same ideas a reality.

This brings a whole new perspective to the genre. It hands it a certain sort of power. Because if science fiction is a reflection of how we see the future, what does that mean for us?

In recent years, science fiction has become synonymous with dystopian. While dystopian fiction is just one of many sub-genres of sci-fi, it really took off in the YA realm, bringing us classics like The Hunger Games, Divergent, The Maze Runner etc. Dystopian stories are a reflection of a collapsed world. They can be quite hopeless even with their revolutionary main characters. Looking at the tyrannical governments, collapsing climates, and humans inability to act humane, it's almost scary how much that's bleeding into reality around us.

So perhaps that's why we love it. We want to see our fears in the stories we read.

Or perhaps we're just that hopeless about the future. Perhaps we only see one future for humanity, one where it eventually kills itself out because there was never another option.

This is why science fiction exists. It's a genre based around options. Some horrifying, some beautiful. I choose to believe we can work towards beautiful stories.

Space opera, for example, is a sub-genre that throws our current state out into the stars. We see spaceships and distant planets where humans exist so humanly. The drama, the mundane nature of it all…all of it so clearly the type of life we lead now, just in another setting.

But my personal favorite is cozy sci-fi. I wrote a book called Moon Soul, and in it I focused on an imperfect utopian moon where humans exist and have struggles, but also do their best to enjoy their lives. I find a lot of hope in stories like this. Stories where authors pour all their aspirations for humanity onto the pages.

The two books that got me into cozy science fiction were Rook Di Goo by Jenni Sauer and The Long Way to a Small, Angry Planet by Becky Chambers. What I loved about both these books was the authentic nature. While the stories felt cozy (mostly due to the character-focused narration), they dealt with real world problems. Some very real problems that really resonated with me.

The truth is, humans will never be perfect. They'll never stop making mistakes. But they'll also never stop being kind and caring and full of dreams. This is the dichotomy of human nature. Even if we get out into the stars, we're going to be human. But it's up to us to decide what types of humans we'll be.

That's why variety in science fiction matters. It gives us something to fight for. We can have our dystopian novels, but we need to balance them out with stories on the other end of the spectrum. Stories that keep us hopeful and excited for what's to come.

When Characters Decide to Twin
By Lori Ann Nelson

Lori Ann Nelson often vanishes into the realms of her imagination where she creates intriguing science fiction worlds or writes posts to fellow chronic illness warriors. She enjoys nature photography and watching old shows. She currently resides in Texas with her family and her German Shepherd mix pup, Viridis.

You have probably discovered by now that you have a thing or two in common with your characters. I'm also sure you can think of a few people who have at least one of the same interests or qualities as you. Just like many people have things in common, some of your characters have mutual attributes with their author. This is part of what helps characters to be relatable. People can relate to characters who leap off the pages with human qualities. You - the author - can give them those qualities because of your past experiences.

But what happens when your character becomes too similar to you? You might notice them taking on the same interests and speech patterns you have. Or maybe they have too many of the same interests and hobbies. Characters that become too much like their authors tend to be a problem. After all, they aren't you.

Each one needs their own identities so they can fit well into their unique stories. Even characters holding a few of your qualities need something you don't have or do that allows them to live in their story world. If you enjoy hockey or digital art, it's kind of hard to have your character doing that in a world where those things might not exist.

So how do we keep our characters from twinning with us? There's a few different ways you can help prevent this!

1: Give Them a Coffee Break

After you identify which character has fallen victim to twinning, write a random scene with them. It doesn't have to be something that will be included in your novel or short story, but it can give you room to better develop their voice without worrying about making edits later. It can be something as random as a trip to a coffee shop or maybe teleporting them to a new city (if you write sci-fi like me).

No matter what your character will be doing, don't worry about the structure of the story yet. Spend that time just focusing on experimenting with your character. Test out their reactions to events or thoughts on something familiar until you feel they have their own voice and personality.

Then resume writing the story with a more solid approach to their character.

2: Create a File for Them!

You know those files hidden in envelopes in the spy movies? Yup! Do that for your character.

Write down everything from their favorite color and food to the more serious things such as weaknesses and relationships with family. Add as many facts as you can think of then include a section about the differences between you and this character.

Write down what fears they have that you don't or things they hate doing that you like (e.g. One of my characters can't stand repairing things such as vehicles, whereas I actually enjoy it). You can even note how they might react to something differently than you would. Perhaps they have the same fear as you but respond differently to it (e.g. The same character I mentioned above tends to freeze completely when facing something bigger than her, while I go quiet to plan my response before acting on it). Anything you jot down will help. A good idea is to keep this close by while you write to make sure they stay consistently true to their identity.

3: INTRODUCE THEM TO A FRIEND!

Sometimes it helps if you can get another set of eyes on your character. So grab a friend and share a snippet of your story with them! They can let you know where you and the character are becoming too alike or if things are going well. If the two of you are too similar, your friend can also help you brainstorm ways to give the character differences again.

If you want feedback as you write, then role playing might be another helpful option. You and your friend choose a character from your own stories, toss one or both of them into a different world, then take turns writing what each character does in response. As you are role playing, you can ask your friend to point out responses and traits that need to be altered before you get back to your project. This method is to be used with a lot of moderation, but some writers find it very helpful when they get stuck.

Another option is to ask your friend to interview your character. You can request they focus on specific topics or anything that comes to mind and you write out a response as if it's your character talking instead of you. This helps you take their development further while practicing their response and thought reactions.

There have been plenty of times I thought I knew my characters well enough or had their history planned out until my characters went through an interview. Then I realized I needed to adjust a few things. And guess what? My characters were even better afterwards because it gave me the chance to add more touches of uniqueness that shined in their stories! As a bonus, it also ensured they weren't too similar to other characters either.

Any way you do it, two heads can be better than one when it comes to characters.

All of these options will work differently for everyone and each writer has their favorites. None of them are meant to replace writing your actual project. It isn't mandatory to use all of these. Tailor them to whatever works for you or find something else entirely. Test each method out until you find one or two that work well. It might even vary from project to project, and that is fine too.

Whatever you choose, characters are a very important part of any story. Don't be nervous to dive deep and write them as the individuals they are! Some will be more like you than others, and that's okay. As I said at the beginning, that is how it goes with people in the real world too. Whoever your characters are, just give them their space to shine!

Publishing Check List!

Think you're ready to indie publish your book? Let's find out!

1) Edit your manuscript as many times as you can (while staying sane!)

2) Find a critique partner, or beta readers to do an initial read for any major problems or improvements. If you're not sure what to ask your beta readers or critique partners, you can do a quick google search for "Questions to Ask Beta Readers" and find lots of great lists.

3) Hire an editor. Even after your own edits and the input of beta readers, you'll still miss some problems only professional editors can pick up! Whether it's for plot, character, development, grammar, or sentence structure, an editor will take your book from feeling amateurish, to being professional.

4) Learn how to format books or hire a formatter. It's very important that you take this step BEFORE getting your book's cover since designers will need to know the spine thickness.

5) Design your cover or hire a designer. You can find hundreds of amazing artists/designers on Instagram or who are talented at covers. Just search: #bookcoverdesigner

6) Research the different distribution companies. Between KDP, Ingramspark, Barnes&Noble, BookBaby, BookVault and more, you'll have plenty of options for printing and distributing your book. Do your research to see which will work best for you.

7) Upload your files and choose a release day!

8) Plan your cover reveal and pre-orders announcement on the same day to maximize sales. Don't forget to let family and friends help you reveal the cover by offering pre-made graphics!

9) Market, market, market your book all the way until release day. Don't stop talking about it!

10) Celebrate on release day! You've just published a book!

Words From the Heart

WHAT I WANT FOR ME

I want you all
to entertain
this simple thought for me.

That, perhaps, instead
of me ruling the world,
I only want you to see,

Sometimes even the fiercest of souls
just wants to simply be.
And that a gentle forest and one quiet love
is all I want for me.

BY EFFIE JOE STOCK

Effie Joe Stock is the author of The Shadows of Light series, creator of the world Rasa, and head of Dragon Bone Publishing. When she's not slaving away in front of her computer, you can find her playing music, studying psychology, theology, or philosophy, playing fantasy RPG video games, riding motorcycles, or hanging out with her farm animals. Her publishing journey only just beginning, Stock looks forward to the release of her fantasy series along with other Dragon Bone titles.

DROWNING UNDER FLAMES

Burning under resentment.
I'm sick of speaking in confrontation,
As if it will heal wounds made in secret.
It hasn't.

Alone in a roomful of people.
Tears rise, I'm drowning.
I wish to die amongst friends,
Only without their judgment.

Dragged under exhaustion.
Yearning for things that once were,
As if happiness existed in them.
It didn't.

I hear them laughing.
The waters rise.
I feel their judgment.
The flames rise.

Instagram: @effie.joe.stock.author
Website: www.effiejoestock.com

Oh Time it Hungers

Time is hungry
it leaves aches
it leaves pain

Time draws creases
across skin
and turns colour
into greys

Time eats minds
crumples memories
vacuums years

you cannot outrun Time
but you can cherish what Time you do have
fold it into your soul

and so allow Time
to nurture
to heal

Time after Time

Kettle

Anger is a privilege
bottling it does curse
so even all that anger
cannot be spent in verse

Sometimes I feel like shouting
sometimes I want to scream
or want to bellow swear words
in a constant fiery stream

I cannot let it out though
all concern for what they'd think
for the fright it might cause others
or for the guilt I'd later bear

To be less afraid
of how I'm perceived
or how other people feel
what a freedom that would be

A. E. Bratchford is a Queer author and poet based in Naarm/Melbourne, Australia. They mostly write and read cosy fantasy/sci-fi, both in poetry and prose. When not writing they are most likely listening to music, going for walks, or drinking tea (or - in some cases - all of the above).

By A. E. Bratchford

Writing in the Dark

A black hole devours
what I write in the dark.
I expect the stories to come true,
horrors of the night
standing just out of view.

Nathaniel Luscombe is an author from Ontario, Canada. When not reading or writing, you can find him thinking about reading and writing. He writes across many genres, has been published in multiple anthologies, and is busy working on more sci-fi and science fantasy works.

Living is more than existing.
It's lining up by the side of the road
because the universe is aligning
and we want to stand in its shadow.

It's staring in awe at the totality
and feeling lost and found
in the beauty of it all.

It's forgetting, just for a minute,
the weight of the burdens
that tie us to this Earth.

By Nathaniel Luscombe

What Could Have Been
By Marion Cedar

What could have been?
Every night,
In the middle of the night,
I lay in bed
Thinking,
Asking myself
Why did I said that?
The words that wounded you,
Even when I didn't really mean them,
And I think of what could have been.
I would be holding your hand,
Getting lost in your blue eyes,
Staring off into the sunset with you,
If I fixed things sooner,

Would it have made your heart beat better?
Would we have been better off?
Maybe you wouldn't have said what you said.
I still don't know if you meant it,
But our eyes still lock at times,
And I wonder what you think.
Do you also lie in bed?
Asking yourself the exact same thing:
What could have been?

Marion always wanted to be a writer. At thirteen, she decided that she wanted to be a published author. While working on her books, she got into poetry. When she isn't writing, you can find her practicing ballroom dancing, painting, or riding her dirt bike.

Interviews with Fellow Writers Passing on their Advice!

Adding Deep Themes to Cozy Stories
With Jenni Sauer & Effie Joe Stock

Jenni Sauer is the creator of Ivory Palace Press and is dedicated to writing fairy tale retellings filled with realism, hope, mental health representation and irresistibly cozy vibes. Her books are full of characters in fantastical worlds struggling with the same difficulties we do on earth and it's her hope that we find little pieces of ourselves in her stories.

I'm Effie Joe Stock and in this interview, I'm diving deep into Jenni's chosen genre and what messages she hopes to convey to her readers.

Q. Jenni, I've read just one of your many works (The Witch at the Edge of the Woods) and was surprised at the emotional depth your writing contains. Why did you decide to write cozy fantasy and how does that relate to you conveying deep messages?

A. For as long as I can remember, I only ever saw myself in characters with tragic endings. There was a hot second in the early 2010's where mental illness representation was on the rise, but it was always in a character who was othered, who was tolerated, and who often met a tragic end of sorts. And as someone who was dealing with a lot of trauma and the overwhelming depression that came with it, it felt like at my darkest, I was bombarded with the message that I was only worthy of a tragic ending.

It is a strange paradox to be an eternal optimist with depression, but as such, I stubbornly refused to believe that message. And I wanted to write books about characters who struggle deeply, but also get to have those cozy, healing moments, whose pain and joy can go hand in hand.

Q. What a beautiful message, and one that's so important for many of us to hear! I once read a post of yours about why you chose to put a girl in a crop top on one of your covers (and why she wears one in the book). Why was this such a pivotal moment for you in your writing career?

A. I have a very complicated relationship with my body, in part due to religious trauma. I spent years of my life as a "skirts only" girl, not due to personal conviction, but because when I was in my darkest, I felt so invisible in the church and hoped if I conformed myself into the perfect Christian girl, people would care about me.

Ziya in a crop top on the front of Kling Klang Gloria is a hug to that younger version of myself, a reminder that it was never about what I was wearing. Fashion has been an amazing tool to help me repair my relationship with my body, but it's also the least interesting thing about myself. I can honor God and be loved by him, I can find my healing, in whatever makes me most comfortable to wear. Some days that's dresses, some days that's crop tops, I'm not more worthy on different days. And it's the girls who feel that same struggle that I want to write stories for. Everyone is welcome in the Evraft Galaxy, but you're going to have to deal with the crop tops while you're here.

Q. As someone who has also dealt with the same religious trauma, hearing you dive into these topics and healing brings me such peace and hope for the next generation! With that in mind, how are you hoping to continue creating stories with emotional depth and what topics are you looking to tackle next?

A. I never really plan what subjects I want to tackle, it's more that they choose me as my stories develop. In The Witch at the Edge of the Woods up until I was writing the end, I would have said Eva's magic didn't symbolize anything. But as the story progressed, I realized how much her relationship with her magic mirrored my own journey in finding the confidence to use my voice and speak up for myself.

I've been focusing on the Thugs and Kisses series recently (a cozy mafia romance series set in the Evraft Galaxy) and something that has crept in is my heroines are all girls who are very confident in what they want and one of the main things they really want is to be kissed by the main character, please and thank you. It's a soft, silly little thing, but as someone who was taught that sort of desire is always shameful, it's been healing to challenge that idea and explore how to include those desires while still writing books that align with my desire to honor God in everything I write.

Q. It's always amazing to see what the subconscious mind works into our writing! And even more amazing when it brings healing to not only other people but also ourselves. Your next project sounds incredible and I'm very impatiently waiting for it now. If you had one last thing to tell your readers or potential readers to close out this interview, what would you tell them?

A. Thank you so much! Since we've talked so much about healing, I'd love to leave readers with a final encouragement that if any of this resonated with you, but you're still struggling to find your way out, it does get better. It still hurts sometimes, some hurts never truly go away. But you learn to live with the hurt and the joy really does get a lot louder than the pain (I know that sounds so fake, but I promise it's true). Healing is one of the hardest things you'll ever do, but it's worth it in the end. You deserve to heal, you deserve to be here, even on the days when it feels like you don't. And you are so worth all the hard work.

And if you need a place to rest for a little while full of hope and healing and broken people who get to live, I hope you'll check out my books; the Evraft Galaxy always welcomes new visitors. I hope you'll stay a while.

Creating in the Face of Adversary
With Nikkita Bell & Effie Joe Stock

Nikkita Bell is an adult paranormal romance author and artist who looks to entertain and inspire others with her dark creativity. Her debut novella Bound in Pincers released early 2024 and despite personal setbacks, Bell is taking the indie publishing world by storm with her label Scorpion Script Press.

I'm Effie Joe Stock and in this interview, I'm diving into Nikkita's creative process and how she overcame staggering difficulties to be where she is today.

Q. Nikkita, I read your first novella, Bound in Pincers when it released early 2024 and fell in love. You seem to gravitate toward sarcastic, sassy characters with a dark side. What draws you to these types of characters?

A. I've always considered myself a funny gal, but I've always been more of an innocent-sweet funny. I've always gravitated towards darker characters who are devastatingly witty and unapologetically themselves, regardless of social norms. I use writing as an outlet or an experiment to tap into a darker side to have a little fun and keep life interesting. I believe my fascination with dark sarcasm stems from Disney villains, specifically Maleficent and Scar, who were the epitome of dark wit!

Q. When did you first discover your love and talent for writing and art? And what inspires you to create?

A. I've been drawing since I was 4 years old. As children, my sister was the writer and I was the illustrator, and our dream was to grow up and publish books that she writes and I illustrate. When I was a teenager, she took me to a bookstore and asked the store owner to pick out a book that was like "raunchy Harry Potter" and they picked out an option for me. It ended up being a book about werewolves and I absolutely fell in love! From that point on, I discovered that I, too, wanted to write. Both of my passions just had to coexist together. And now I do both.

Q. That is such a hilarious and heartwarming story! I know you dealt with some extremely difficult setbacks earlier this year. How did those obstacles affect your writing?

A. In February of this year, I developed acute kidney failure and was comatose for 4 days as a result. When I woke up, they told me my kidneys would never work again and I'd need dialysis indefinitely. Longest story short, my kidneys and I kicked total ass and bounced back completely and I am currently (as of August 29) 6 months dialysis free! This entire experience was grueling for my creative side. The physical recovery took a couple months, but mental recovery is still something I am dealing with everyday. I felt like I was unable to create, could not tal into that part of my brain and worried that I'd never have the desire to write or draw ever again. But finally, in late June, the spark returned. And it all started from playing a little Baldur's Gate 3. Before I knew it, I started coming up with new projects and ideas for the next year.

Q. I can't even imagine how hard it was to grapple such a terrifying illness. In regard to your mental healing, how does that affect your creative process now vs before and what is some advice you have for others who may also be struggling with physical ailments that might be blocking their creativity?

A. The best advice I can offer anyone is to give yourself TIME! Everyone's healing process is different and the timeline doesn't matter. Sometimes, the spark doesn't come back for years. Sometimes, it comes back immediately. I found that writing down all my feelings really helped me come to terms with what I went through, and some days, reading back on those thoughts helps me recognize my strength. I think what also really worked for me was trying to take my situation and see what types of ways I can use it to be advantageous to me. For instance, how can I include the feelings I felt during this life event and add it to my story? How can I accurately depict fears, sorrows, and even triumphs in my writing?

Mental healing doesn't take weeks or months, it can take years. And some days, I feel like I'm back to square one. But reminding myself to take one day at a time, be kinder to myself about timelines and setting realistic goals makes all the difference. It's okay to not have an awesome and productive day every day. Sometimes, it's great to just wake up and enjoy the simple pleasures.

Q. You've truly overcome so much in the last few months. I know I'm the only one happy to see you back on your feet, not only because you're such an incredible human being but also because we want to see what you create next! You mentioned new projects. What can we look forward to in the next year?

A. My current project (and in my eyes, magnum opus), is finishing the draft of my debut novel, The Bombshell Devil's Advocate, a gothic noir dark urban fantasy set to release early in 2025! It is an expanded, rewritten, and retconned version of my first novella, Bound in Pincers, where we follow my character, October Winters, a dark witch bound to the Devil, who is faced with the ultimatum of a lifetime. And if that wasn't enough, the book is getting over 30 fully illustrated comic-style companion pages with each chapter!

I'm truly overwhelmed with the scope of your next project and am waiting on pins and needles for it! Thank you so much for sharing with us your writing process, and offering advice for those who may be struggling with their own overwhelming obstacles. Your story is truly an inspiration and I know it will help encourage many other writers in their own journey.

The Church of St. Jonah
By Jess Autiero

Jess is an Italian author situated in Sweden. When they're not working as a teacher, they're often found daydreaming, drinking an unhealthy dose of tea, and annoying their cats for some love. They've self-published a supernatural novel in May 2023, and are now working on two fantasy novels.

Insagram: @autierowrites

I never considered myself a person of faith. The concept of organised religion did not resonate with me; I never stepped foot inside a church or attended a mass, and I remained sceptical of the myriad gods humanity has invented over the centuries. Even when I travelled, I purposely tried to avoid areas known for their religious significance. I entrusted that territory to a colleague, allowing me the freedom to explore and critique other aspects of culture and history of a place without that obligation hanging over me.

Spenselbridge, a rather anonymous village in the heart of the British countryside, was my last assignment. Tasked with the inglorious duty of penning a review of this secluded place for my travel guide company, I couldn't suppress my indignation to the meaning behind this travel.

In the prime days of an agent's career, Barcelona, San Francisco, Tokyo and the most popular cities of the world were assigned, with promises of endless activities and entertainment. As the agent aged, more sombre were the destinations. Rome, Venice, Prague, cities full of history and culture, of good food and wine. And as the years went by, so did the decline in allure, until one found themselves dispatched to remote and forgotten corners of the world. The subtle but unmistakable message from our company that our services were no longer needed.

My last gift before retirement. Not that I wanted to, but who cares what an old man wants, right?

The notebook laid open in front of me, a few scribbles on a mostly white page. This village had no history, no art, and certainly no peculiar remarks. That, added to the knowledge of this being my last assignment, made the task even more arduous to overcome.

"Hello darling! What can I get for you?"

As I tore my fatigued eyes from the almost empty page, I was met by the most beautiful amber eyes I had ever seen in my entire life. Even in the light dim of the pub, they were splendid. I felt more inspired to write an ode to her eyes than anything about that insipid village.

"Are you a journalist?" she asked, her voice soft but full of life.

"No, I am a writer. I write for a travel guide company, Wander Wings. Have you heard of them?"

"Wicked! Alas no, I have no use for travel guides. I've never been outside the village." She shrugged, her brown curls bobbing around her. At that, I was left speechless. I had never in my life met anyone who did not travel.

"That can't be possible! Not even to London? Or the next village?"

"No, is that so surprising? I have everything I need right here. Why would I need to go anywhere else?"

A sarcastic laugh escaped my lips before I could stop it. "Really?" I asked, turning my whole attention to her. "I have travelled and been everywhere, and no offence, but it seems like I could hardly find anything here at all."

"Oh, ye of little faith!" she giggled. That was the cutest sound I had ever heard, and I wanted to experience it again.

"Say, the place is almost empty… would you care to join me for a pint?" I motioned towards the chair in front of me.

She smiled, eyes sparkling with something mysterious and intriguing. "Let me take your order, and I'll gladly join you."

She quickly turned, and I couldn't help but look at her forms. She was gorgeous. When she turned, she caught me staring, and I quickly averted my eyes.

She joined me at the table, pushing a pint of copper beer towards me.

"Like what you see?" she asked in a sensual voice.

I coughed, slightly embarrassed, and took my beer. "I apologise if I made you feel uncomfortable. I must admit, though, that you are a beautiful woman."

Her giggle returned, eyes sparkling with playfulness, and once again I stared at her. A stutter in my heart, like a flame once again rekindled, made me lean towards her.

"Ta. I take great pride in keeping my body in shape, despite my age."

"Your age? Why, you are so young! In your forties, I presume."

That made her burst into laughter, and I could swear my heart sang at that sound. I felt like a teenager again, crushing hard on an almost perfect stranger.

"You are such a tease! I'm fifty-four." Her hand sliding on my arm, she winked.

"Fifty-four? Impossible!" I exclaimed, my voice higher than I would have liked. "I am fifty-six, and I look like I could be your older brother, if not your father." I leaned in. "Don't tell me you have found the Fountain of Youth in this secluded village, for I will never believe you."

"You are such a charmer, aren't you?" she winked again, and took a sip from her Cola.

I took the chance to do the same with my beer. As the copper liquid met my tongue, I was overwhelmed by how light it was on the palate, with flavours that hinted at summer and a subtle reminiscence of its flowers. And as it travelled to my stomach, a sense of tranquillity and peace took over me.

"Oh, my, what an unexpected flavour!"

"It's our local beer, our signature if you'd like. Saint Jonah's beer, we call it."

"Never heard of it, and never tasted something like this. May I inquire about the name?"

"It is in honour of our local Saint and Protector, St. Jonah. When the first followers of St. Jonah came here, they built a chapel on what is now the outskirts of town. The monks produced the beer to attract more people here, and of course as a way to help the community. You could write that in your guide." She tapped gently on the notebook, and thanking her I scribbled a few notes down.

"Now that I think of it - I was almost forgetting, what a perfect timing! Tonight is our chapel's anniversary! This is the most important event here in Spenselbridge. You should come with me!" The excitement in her voice was cut short by what I suppose was my grimace.

"What's the problem?"

"I tend to avoid churches and all of that." I shrugged, trying to feel less guilty as I looked into her sad eyes. "I'm not a believer, and I'm afraid my knowledge of saints, patrons and gods is limited by my childhood curiosity."

I braced myself for the plethora of questions I was sure would erupt from her any seconds. That was what typically happened every time I disclosed my lack of faith, each one more irksome than the previous. However, she didn't flinch. Her smile grew back, and her eyes sparkled with playfulness.

"You know," she said after a while. "I didn't catch your name. I'm Susan. Susan Pepperday."

Smiling, I shook her soft hand. "I think we skipped the introductions. William Evans. Billy for my friends."

"Billy," she replied, and my name said from those lips made me shiver. "Say, Billy, let's make a deal. You come with me to the celebrations, so you have something to write for your guide, and afterwards we could come back here and have a pint… or something else, if you'd like." Her long nails gently grazed my arm, and I felt my body warming up at her touch. I leaned in, and smiled.

"Deal."

As Susan had already disclosed, the chapel was on the outskirts of the village. Its off-white exterior shimmered under the almost full moon. Small-scaled, squared, its tower no higher than three metres. Nothing peculiar about it screamed 'tourist attraction', but in lack of anything else to write about, I noted down on my trusted notepad a first impression of the chapel, sure that I would reformulate and embellish it later. It looked like no more than twenty, maybe thirty people could squeeze in it, and yet more people that I could count were lining up to enter it, the terrain around it filled with cars.

I glanced at Susan, curiosity taking over my skepticality. She had changed into light jute robes, a traditional robe worn on that day specifically, and had instructed me to wear my most light-coloured clothes. I had opted for a white shirt and khaki trousers.

She looked at me with a glint in her eyes that I hardly recognised, but before I could inquire she took my hand and quickened her steps.

"Don't stop, the ceremony is about to start!"

We were squeezed inside the wooden frames, and there I found the secret. The church was completely desert, save for the people queuing along the rail of what I supposed was a staircase to an underground chapel. People around us ignored me, but exchanged smiles with Susan. I started down the stairs following my companion, and only after what felt like an eternity we reached the bottom. Susan glanced at me in the dark vestibule, her eyes sparkling in the lights of the candles.

"Welcome to the Church of St. Jonah!" she spoke in hushed anticipation, as her firm hand dragged me through the door leading into the next room.

As my eyes adjusted to the sudden brightness, my mind had trouble taking in the view. The creamy-white stone walls, flanked by towering columns, stretched skywards. Any other grandiose building had suddenly paled in comparison to the magnificence of this church despite its absence of decorations. Mouth agape, I suddenly felt very insignificant.

But what truly captured my attention, as I finally acclimatised with the view, was at the pinnacle of the central nave. There, suspended by thick ropes that reached up to the very high of the church roof, was a massive whale, its skin glowing an ethereal blue.

Words tried to form in my mouth, but not even a peep came out of it.

"Isn't it marvellous?" Susan's excited voice pulled me back from my trance.

"Why is there a taxidermied whale on the roof?" I blurted out, stunned, unsure if left speechless by the building itself or the bizarre peculiarity that hovered over us.

Susan just laughed, and tugged me again.

I let her, my mind too startled to do anything but. Only when we finally sat down I was able to tear my eyes away from the whale. Barely. As I forced myself to keep my eyes down, I noticed that we were very close to the first row. I turned, and studied the myriad of people sitting behind us.

"Where do all these people come from?" I whispered to Susan.

"This is a very sacred tradition. People flow from all around the world to come back and celebrate our Patron and Saviour."

I slowly turned to face her. A creeping sensation was gnawing at me, a hunch that I was missing a piece of vital information. Something was going on. The forgotten notepad pressed uncomfortably in my back pocket as my palms began sweating with unease. Before I could utter another word, a bell rang, its clear sound hushing any and every sound in the church.

An older couple, a man and a woman, both wearing the same light jute robes but adorned with gold embroidery around the edges and a golden belt on their waist, stood at the altar.

"Brothers and sisters, today we gather to celebrate and honour the Patron of our existence, the cornerstone of our congregation. Year after year, we gather here in this hallowed place to remember and pay homage to the one who bestowed upon us our sacred obligation in His divine name. Our heart fills with joy as we witness the familiar faces of our faithful brethren, and we want to extend a warm welcome to those who join our humble family here today. Welcome to all!"

The church erupted in cheers and applause, and I felt hands on my shoulder and gentle pats on my back from those around me. I couldn't help but feel bewildered at the sudden attention.

Leaning into Susan, I whispered, "Should I tell them I'm only here to write an article?"

She glanced at me with something in her eyes that made me move back. "Don't worry about that now, and keep watching."

Every single cell was urging me to move, to run away from that creepiness that was slowly but surely saturating the air around me. Frozen, I couldn't do anything but keep silent, the uneasiness building up in my whole body.

"As is customary, before we begin our celebrations and praises to our great St. Jonah, we partake in the same meat that sustained Him during His time of Repentance! We kindly request those seated in the middle of the nave to make way. We want to ensure that no one is caught in the procession. However, should such event take place, it might be deemed as part of St. Jonah's divine plan."

Laughters scattered around me, even from Susan's lips, but the edge in her shrilling voice had me tremble.

"Susan, I don't-" but before I could utter another word, a piercing sound boomed around us. I shot my eyes upward and, to my horror, I witnessed the impossible: the whale was moving. And not because it was slowly descending towards us. Its tail thrashed, trying to find an escape to the tight ropes that bound her. Then it sang the most haunting melody I had ever experienced. A mournful, desperate lament that paralysed my body and shattered my heart. Terror gripped me as I was trying to comprehend the incomprehensible.

"Is there something wrong, my dear?" Susan's voice was a gentle knife in the noise, her hands slowly enwrapping me. "Isn't it splendid?"

"I need to get out." I had never sounded so terrified in my whole life. "I must get out."

"But, Billy dear, what about our promise?"

"Fuck your promise!" I blurted out. "You never told me this was a cult! A depraved, deranged cult. I'm leaving now."

As I stood, the same gentle hands that cheered on me before reappeared, holding me in a grip that tightened by the instant. Pain shot into my limb as I tried to flight, and the pressure intensified.

Susan's gaze met mine, her eyes strangely calm and devoid of any surprise at my distress.

"But Billy, you can't leave us now." She said, inching closer. "You are a sign from our great Jonah! Never has such an opportunity been presented to us. You have been chosen, my dear Billy, to spread His message far and wide! You have been chosen by His Grace alone! It is your duty on this Earth!"

"What are you talking about?" I shouted, panic and anger equally swelling up in my chest. "Sign? Duty? I don't believe in this shit! Let me go!"

Susan smiled again, gently. "Don't worry, my dear. You'll soon understand."

I thrashed, my screams filling up the church. She turned, and calmly reached for the whale that had descended but a metre from the ground. Her fingers caressed the whale's dark skin, before her fingers dug into its side. I watched, transfixed with disgust, as her bloody hand came out, a chunk of the whale's meat between her fingers. As more people reached out to do the same, pressing the meat into their craving mouths, the whale's wretched song resonated among the walls right into my bones.

For a moment, the whale's gaze met mine, desperation reflected in both of us.

We were both trapped.

As Susan turned to me, hand outstretched, I tried a desperate last stand against all that madness. Fingers dug into my body, as I felt my bones on the verge of breaking.

"Hush now, my dear," Susan cooed, her calmness unnerving me every instant more. "Don't fret about it. The meat is not spoiled, if that's what distresses you. The whale, you see, is cursed to endure eternal regeneration. It cannot die as long as the Church of St. Jonah survives. It grants us the privilege to partake in its flesh, as it once feasted upon the sacred body of our Jonah."

Her approach was slow and deliberate, her smile never faltering. "Once you taste it, you will be enlightened! You'll understand your rightful position on Earth, and fulfil your mission."

The crimson meat was pressed on my face, its warmth nauseating me. Lips sealed, I swayed my head, unconcerned to the blood smearing my face as long as that thing didn't get in.

Susan's lips lost the gentle smile, and edge of displeasure now contouring her face. "Jonah disapproves of those who seek to avoid their mission." She said, stern, as one of her fingers clawed my lips and pulled up high. My mouth was unfastened, and she pushed the flesh on my tongue.

Silence of Sleep in a Forest So Deep

(A Rasaverse Story)
By Effie Joe Stock

Website: www.effiejoestock.com
Insagram: @effie.joe.stock.author

Effie Joe Stock is the author of The Shadows of Light series, creator of the world Rasa, and head of Dragon Bone Publishing. When she's not slaving away in front of her computer, you can find her playing music, fantasy RPG video games, riding motorcycles, or hanging out with her farm animals. Her publishing journey only just beginning, Stock looks forward to the release of her fantasy series along with other Dragon Bone titles.

Trans-Falls, Ravenwood

Year: Rumi 5209 Q.RJ.M

Many creatures enter forests hoping to find solace and silence, but those who live in the woods know silence is the sound of death. For Keziah, the oppressive silence was the most wretched thing she'd ever heard.

Stepping gingerly over sticks and fallen branches, Keziah avoided stepping on anything that would shatter the silence. As much as she hated it, she felt it'd be blasphemous to disrupt it. She wasn't the only one; she'd seen the other Centaurs avoiding the stone walkways throughout Trans-falls lest their hooves clatter against them. The city itself seemed dead in the silence, and out here in the thick of the woods, Keziah was painfully aware of how very alone she was—how very alone they all were.

Eyes catching sight of a blue shimmer, Keziah changed her path and picked her way to the small growth of elusive zheborgiy fungus. They were higher up the tree trunk than she could reach. Painfully, she remembered how easy it used to be to simply ask the tree for help. Now when she looked at the bark, it remained lifeless, motionless, as still as death. Pressing a hand to the tree's rough skin, she wondered if it could feel her still or if it was completely lost in the dark world of sleep.

"Forgive me," she whispered before rearing up, hooves landing against the bark as she reached for the mushrooms. A little farther … Just barely, her fingers wrapped around the shrooms, and she pulled, separating them from their life source. A shiver ran down her spine as she dropped back to the ground, tucking the fungus into her herb basket. It felt wrong to take from the tree without asking first.

But now she didn't have any way of speaking to them, not since …

A wave of naseua washed over her as memories she'd rather not remember flooded her mind.

The sky had been dark for days, throwing Trans-Falls into chaos and disorder. Armies of Warriors had been sent out to find the cause of the darkness. Ambassadors from all over Ventronovia had rushed to find the source. They'd found it had started in the heart of Ravenwood by a Centaur Trans-Falls had called their own.

Bumps rose along Keziah's arm, and she shivered, though the breeze was warm. On the last day of darkness, the sky had rent open. Beings with unfathomable, shifting forms, frighteningly similar to the Etas, moved through the sky, waiting to cross the gap between Rasa and Hanluurasa, the sky realm. Hundreds of eyes had shone down, watching, waiting, full of hunger. Then a wave of magic exploded across the land, bending trees, tearing apart homes, and even killing several Centaurs.

One moment, the forest had been alive and teeming with nymphs, Fauns, and walking trees. The next, they were all gone.

Tears collected in Keziah's eyes as she remembered watching the forest slip beneath the Sleeping, how she'd run to Phyllida's tree and watched as her nymph friend curled into its roots, closed her eyes, and promised she was only taking a nap. Keziah hadn't seen her since.

When the memories faded, Keziah found herself staring at the same tree—a delicate weeping willow with long, spindly branches flowing in the breeze. No other movement rippled through its boughs.

Ducking under the strings of leaves and branches, Keziah dragged her hooves to the tree's trunk, touching the bark where Phyllida's face had once been with petals for eyes and leaves for lips. Now it was faceless—no different than any other nymph-less tree.

"When will you wake? How long will I have to wait?"

Before the Sleeping, Keziah had spent her days running through the forest with Phyllida, chasing handsome tree nymphs, swimming in the streams with the river nymphs, and collecting ingredients for Keziah's healing class. They'd been young, carefree back then, hardly worrying about the state of the world, simply making the most of each warm sun ray and cold river.

In one day, Keziah had been forced to grow up, to leave behind the childish laughter and games. As a healer, she'd been called to duty for Trans-Falls. The Sleeping hadn't just affected the forest; it'd damaged the Centaurs as well. After all, the trees and Fauns were brethren to the Centaurs. Now she spent almost all her free time tending to those weakened by the curse hanging over the forest.

Her fingers tightened around the blue zheborgiy fungus she'd collected. It seemed such a small amount compared to the hundreds who lay sick or wounded and in need of ingredients like it. She was lucky she was young; the older Centaurs like her father hadn't been able to recover from the dark magic's presence as quickly; some hadn't survived at all.

Trying to keep her hands from shaking, Keziah removed three small Leño-zhego flowers from her basket and laid them at the base of the tree. "I know you're only sleeping, but it feels like you've died." Though she knew an answer wouldn't come, disappointment stabbed her heart with the silence anyway. "But that's alright. I promise I'll be here when you wake up. The Igentis is already looking for the Zelauwgugey, the Lyre of the Forest's Essence. He says it could bring you back. I know it will." She pressed her lips to the trunk, smelling the wood, the leaves, and wishing she could smell the blossoms that once grew in the leaves. "Soon. We'll be together again soon."

Turning, she ducked back under the willowing branches, believing for a moment that they wrapped around her a little tighter, as if holding her there. Then they fell lifeless again. Swallowing her hope, Keziah walked back into the forest to finish collecting the ingredients she would need for her dark magic repelling potion her father needed. All the while, she whispered the potion's spell under her lips, searching for the small magic residing in her mind. The more she practiced, the stronger she could make the potion and the more likely her father was to recover—the more likely all the older Centaurs were to recover.

They needed to survive, they needed to carry on the stories of the forest, to speak of a time when the trees waved their branches like arms, laughed with breath smelling of sap and spring, and how their spirits would step from their physical bodies and run through the forest, making mischief, and blessing the land with new growth wherever they crossed. Someone needed to speak of the Fauns and their wild parties, and the beat of their drums, and the trill of their flutes. Someone needed to carry stories and legends they told of great beings who once walked Rasa and Hanluurasa, shaping the very world and sky, and of star beings who came down from Haluurasa to fuse their spirits into the forest.

Keziah tightened her fists with determination. Though the forest was as silent as death now, it didn't have to stay that way … not forever. Until someone found the Zelauwgugey Lyre and banished the dark magic, Keziah promised to bring the noise back, to bring the life back.

As she made her way home, she walked on the stone road, hooves striking loudly against the rock, echoing through the silent forest. In the distance, she almost believed she heard a Faun's drum answer.

Resources

Find the Freelancer You and Your Book Need

Artists/Designers

CaffeinateArt

I create character illustrations for book covers and marketing material with a specialty in the fantasy genre.

Instagram: @CaffeinateArt

Kate Korsak | Fantasy Cartographer

hiiiii my name is kate and I make fantasy maps! I'm an indie author who got into fantasy cartography as a way to bring my own worlds to life. I found that I loved creating new worlds and mapping them, and eventually decided to offer cutsom maps to other worldbuilders!

I make maps for:
- authors
- homebrew RPGs
- any fantasy world you want mapped!

please be sure to read the terms before commissioning me!!

Website: ko-fi.com/katekorsak
Instagram: @writerkatek

Gardens Book Design

Offering affordable, professional cover and logo design for indie/small press authors. Whether you need a cover for your first novel or a remodel for your published series, we're here to help!

Instagram: @gardensbookdesign
Website:
https://abbyelissaauthor.wixsite.com/abby-johansen---auth/services-4

MoonPress Design

Hello! I'm Bianca and I'm a book cover designer based in Atlanta, GA. As a professional cover designer, I've been able to work with bestselling authors, publishing houses and indie authors on a variety of different projects and genres. Being able to connect and work with professionals in the writing industry is one of the best parts of the cover design business! I specialize in creating designs for covers that meet their expectations as well as the current market standard.

Instagram: @moonpressdesign

Sakura Artist

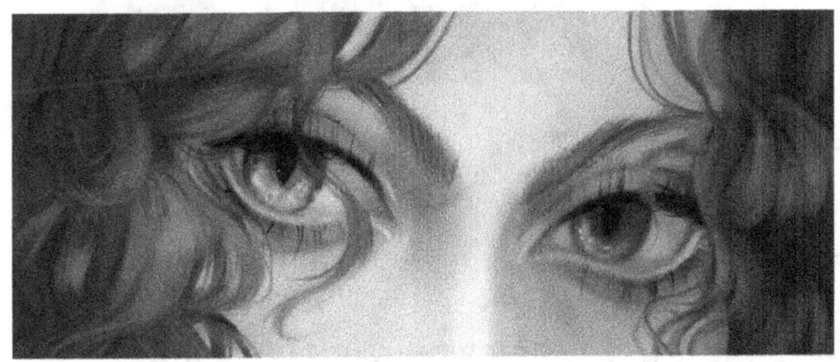

Amelia • 28 • Freelance Illustrator
Co-Creator of @ahcomicmagic
Illustrator for 'The Safekeepers' on Webtoons

Website: https://linktr.ee/Sakuraartist
Instagram: @sakuraartist

Small Press/Publications

Luna Publishing Consulting LLC

Our small press is dedicated to publishing diverse and compelling voices in contemporary fiction and poetry. We specialize in helping writers bring their stories to life through personalized publishing services, from manuscript editing and cover design to marketing strategies. As a woman-owned business, our mission is to empower emerging and underrepresented authors, offering them the platform and support they need to reach a wider audience. We're passionate about nurturing talent and committed to fostering a vibrant literary community. We are currently accepting submissions from authors seeking a publishing partner who values creativity and originality.

At our publishing consulting company, we specialize in guiding authors through the entire publishing process. We offer a range of services tailored to your needs, including manuscript editing and formatting, book cover design, ISBN creation, and personalized marketing strategies. Whether you're pursuing self-publishing or traditional publishing, our expert team provides professional, a la carte services to ensure your book reaches its full potential. We're committed to helping you navigate the complexities of publishing, so you can focus on what matters most—your writing. Let us turn your dreams into polished, market-ready pages.

Website: https://lunapublishingllc.com/
Instagram: @lunapublishingllc

This small publishing house was founded by author @mkahearn. books and specializes in themed fantasy anthology books.
See their website for submission opportunities along with their previously published works.

Website: https://azalapress.com/
Instagram: @azalapress

Azala Press

Quill and Flame Publishers

We publish books aimed at a YA and NA audience--all with romance, but romance that doesn't go beyond a PG-13 level. We accept any genre so long as the book stays within our guidelines. Our regular submission windows fall during the months of January and July. We regularly have open submissions for various anthologies.

Website: https://quillandflame.com/
Instagram: @quill.and.flame.publishers

Editors

CLEVER CROW

I'm Natalie, the clever crow behind Clever Crow. I'm an editor who supports self-published authors in delivering sparkling stories. From developmental editing, to line editing, to proofreading - I am here to support you throughout your self-publishing journey. I offer free sample editing up to 2,000 words so that you can get a feel for how I work well before we sign a contract. I welcome all fiction genres and love chatting with potential clients about their unique project. Get in touch today to find out how I can support you.

Website: www.clevercrow.co.uk
Instagram: @clever.crow.copyediting

MENDELL STUDIOS

I. Love. What. I. Do. Working with authors to help them bring their stories to life is a true joy— and I do my very best to ensure that my authors feel my joy throughout the project!
Not only will you have my utmost respect, commitment to the craft of writing, technical prowess, and extensive expertise in character development, but you'll have a new friend with whom you'll complete the journey. Let's write together!
Editor & Copywriter || fantasy, Christian fiction, and nonfiction/theology || Developmental edits || Line & copy edits|| Theological development

Website: www.mendellstudios.com
Instagram: @mendellstudios

E.A. WHYTE

Website:
www.eawhyte.com/editing-services

I offer editing services for young adult and adult novels, specializing in the genres of fantasy and science fiction. Contact via email for inquires regarding developmental edits, line edits, and manuscript critiques or query and synopsis edits. (Payment plans up to 12 months available.)

BEYOND THE STARS PRESS

I offer editorial services and book coaching. My specialties are science fiction, horror, and fantasy, and I offer copy editing, line editing, proofreading, and developmental editing services. I also offer conlang creation services, creating languages and scripts that suit your bookish needs.

Instragram: @seraamoroso
Website:
https://seraamoroso.wixsite.com/seraamoroso

Editor H. A. Pruitt

Website contact page:
https://www.hapruitt.com/contact

I provide editing services for authors working on their manuscripts. For $0.008 per word, I provide developmental editing, content editing, copyediting, and proofreading (two rounds of editing). I am open to all genres except horror and erotica, and I am open to hard topics but will not accept manuscripts with excessive cursing, sexual content, or gore. If you have any questions, please ask.

Jon Tilton's Editing Services

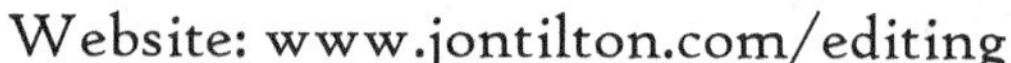

Editing that will take your writing to the next level! Jon doesn't just edit your work, he also explains the "why" behind his suggestions. His notes are more than a simple list of changes—they're also a guide to improve your writing, tailored to your personal strengths and weaknesses. As an independent author himself, Jon understands your need to make every dollar count. You will receive detailed notes covering your manuscript from every angle. Each edit also includes optional phone time to discuss your work. FREE sample edit available upon request. Book your next developmental or line edit today!

Website: www.jontilton.com/editing

DUST AND CROWN
BY HAVELAH MCLAT

Instagram:
@havelahmclatwriter
Buy Now on Amazon

A wicked ruler takes the throne, the fairy kingdom is in chaos, and the dust tree that sustains the fairies is dying.

Fyodar believes Nastia is the only one who can save the kingdom, but Nastia's memory is gone and she can't even remember who she is.

Will they survive the dangerous journey to search for her identity? If so, what will it cost her?

FABLES OF HOPE AND LIGHT
BY HAVELAH MCLAT

Instagram:
@havelahmclatwriter
Buy Now on Amazon

Hardships can be found anywhere. On royal grounds and in the countryside. Inside dreams and books. Perhaps in another realm or on a golden road. Despite the location—trust, courage, and love can always be found to overcome adversity. A group of authors have come together, alongside Havelah McLat and editor Jannette Fuller, to share their heartwarming and whimsical stories. This collection of contemporary and fantasy stories is a must-read for those in need of hope along with a touch of the fantastical.

THE MOON RUN
BY KATHLEEN CONTINE

Finley Clarke swore off racing after a fatal crash cost her first place and her teammate. As she comes around to the idea of entering again, she finds out the only person who is willing to be her new co-pilot is the man named Garis who caused the crash.

As Finley and Garis enter The Moon Run, they realize there's more than just the harsh desert out to get them. The other racers will stop at nothing to win. Even if it means they have to kill. Can Finley and Garis put aside their past to win the race?

Website: KathleenContine.com

A Compendium of Crimes
by Yvanka Maria Guia Rebelo

Dive into a world of intrigue and adventure with 'A Compendium of Crimes: A Cozy Mystery Anthology'

Welcome to a collection of cozy mysteries where diverse settings, unique characters, and captivating plots create an enchanting reading experience.

Featuring stories from talented authors across the globe, this anthology offers something for every mystery lover.

From pulse-pounding thrillers to charming cozy mysteries, sci-fi crimes to Victorian-era detectives, romantic conundrums to paranormal pilferers, each story promises to intrigue and entertain.

Get ready to curl up with a cup of tea and enjoy these delightful mysteries.

Instagram: @a.quiver.of.tales
Buy Now on Amazon

The Woman of Blythe Manor
by Miriam Wade

After a decade away, Luanna Underwood is back in Bramblewood Bay, performing with the local ballet company. Reunited with her childhood best friend Caesar and his college roommates Gavin and Damien, Luanna must uncover the truth behind the haunting of Blythe Manor and confront the ghosts of their pasts and not all of them are dead.

Buy Now on Amazon

Away From Grace
by Jessica Autiero

The Archangel Michael had one mission: to stop Lucifer from fleeing Hell. At any cost. He would have never thought that the price of his failure would have been his own existence.

Trapped in a young human body, deprived of his immortality, powers, and everything that made him an Archangel, Michael finds himself with a new life he never wanted, vowing not to meddle with angelic wars anymore.
Yet, when a tragedy occurs, he has second thoughts. Will Michael have the courage to become the Protector of Humankind once again? And will he have what it takes to move against the creature that he loves more than anything?

Insagram: @autierowrites
Buy Now on Amazon

Like Courage on a Starless Night
by Stacy Bair Ogden

Instagram:
@authorstacybairogden

Naya Gavi has no permanent home, no place to claim as her own. After years of searching, she may have found the home she has been desperately longing for– within Mendlewyn, a lush land in the south of Gnareth. As she navigates the nuisances of maintaining the castle's library, she forges friendships and accidentally stumbles across a plot that could potentially destroy all her hard-fought dreams.

Cursed with a fiery temper, Benjamin Lamar, nephew to the king of Mendlewyn, has until his eighteenth birthday to prove he can change for the better and rise above the taint of embarrassment his anger has caused. Amid his lessons, he catches wind of dangerous secrets and gets caught up in a wave of peril.

The capital city is in danger and it's up to a cautious servant girl, an angry nobleman and their allies to stop their enemies before it's too late.

The first installment of The Gnareth Chronicles, an epic trilogy.

All That There Is(n't) To Know About Frogs
by Amelia E. Clawford

Critics have called this book "utterly useless" and "infuriatingly inaccurate." Within its pages, multi-award-losing scientist Amelia E. Clawford presents a guide to all the facts she made up instead of actually doing research on the topic. Blatantly false, laughably contradictory, and entirely void of anything close to actual insight, All That There Is(n't) To Know About Frogs will equip you with nothing you have ever needed to know about frogs.

Instagram: @amelias.little.library
Buy Now on Amazon

There Will Be Wolves
Compiled by AudraKate Gonzalez

Under the glow of the full moon's light, a symphony of howls pierces the night. But don't be fooled with their hypnotic lures, for in the shadows....there will be wolves.

Instagram: @twenty_hills

P(I)E(A)CE OF MY MIND:
A Poem Book by D. Lisette

In "P(i)e(a)ce of My Mind," D. Lisette invites readers into her battle with suicidal thoughts and demonic nightmares. This raw, honest narrative explores her struggle to hold onto faith in Jesus Christ amidst overwhelming darkness. With the help of therapy, a strong support system, and her deepening relationship with God, she uncovers hope in the faintest whispers. This poignant story offers insights into the connection between mental health and spirituality, serving as a testament to the resilience of the human spirit and the enduring power of faith, even in the darkest moments.

Instagram: @d.lisette.poetry
Buy Now on Amazon

THE ROOTS TRILOGY
BY ANNE ELIZABETH

THE SHADOWS OF THE PAST HAUNT THE PRESENT

Portals into alternate worlds throw Juliet Barrows illusion of an idyllic life upside down. Political intrigue, espionage, heists, and rebellion throw her down a path she had never expected. The challenges Juliet faces now dwarf any she has faced before. Impending danger, difficult decisions, and shadow-forces dog her path. Before long, Juliet realizes that facing her fears and uncertainties is the only way to survive the future, endure the present, and overcome the past.

Instagram @anneelizabethwrites
Website: https://linktr.ee/anneelizabethwrites

SOCIETY SECRETS
BY ELSA L. SINGER

"Matthew Reynolds, Age 40, Father of five, Murdered by an Agent of RASR." Two years later, Kurt Reynolds has been sent off to live in Sayleth City to attend the best military academy in the country. But while he's there he gets roped into a new war, one that'll change the country forever, but the question is... For better or for worse?

Instagram: elsas.galacticvoyages
Buy Now on Amazon

THE LEGENDS OF ARCADIA
BY MORGAN HUBBARD

The Cruel Prince meets Teen Wolf in this immersive, high-stakes original legend. An atmospheric and cozy fantasy trilogy, discovering what it means to be human. Full of shapeshifters and magical creatures from a mix of Celtic and Appalachian folklore, this whimsical tale weaves a story of family with themes of light and truth. Embark on a journey with Eden and Silas challenging stereotypes, stepping into destiny, and overcoming fear.

Instagram: @morganhubbardauthor
Buy Now on Amazon, Barnes&Noble, or Bookshop.org

THE DRACON CHARMERS
OF NIHM: DARK
BY ELLE DOYENNE

In the world of Nihm, magic reigns in a complex hierarchy of 15 elven races spread out over an immensely detailed land that houses all manner of mythical beings; dragons held above all others and known as Sky Guardians. Each book within this world takes you through a major journey in each dragon's long lifespan where you encounter Dracon Charmers, soul-bound as their Dragon Champions. Every journey guides you through knowledge about the Nihm world; its magic system, intricate mythologies observed by its people, and a thrilling history sure to enrapture a fantastical mind.

Facebook: Elle Doyenne
Buy Now on Amazon

RULE 25: DON'T FALL FOR THE TARGET
BY CHARLEIGH FREDERICK

In RULE 25: DON'T FALL FOR THE TARGET, 17 year old Autumn gets her first solo mission. Born into the head of one of the world's four largest crime families, Autumn's future seemed predetermined.

But the 24 rules that ran her life since birth begin to feel confining instead of guiding. And when she meets Kato, the boy she's supposed to target for her first solo mission, will the rule book save her life or give her a new one? She never thought she would need to add another rule to her family manifesto. After meeting Kato, she's not so sure.

Instagram & Tiktok: @author_charleighfred
Buy Now on Amazon & Barnes&Noble

Sanded Soul
by Tori Diederich Lundell

A harsh punishment is cast upon Morpheus, the god of dreams, by the Night Council. He caused an imbalance in the world and must now roam the earth endlessly as the Sandman. Placing his sanded palm over the eyes of those who sleep, he brings dreams to all who have lost hope during WWII. Klara, an unexpected visitor from Germany, is somehow able to enter his dreamworld, breaking the lonely chains that bind him. They must find a way to battle the evil that taints the existence of humanity.

Drawn into an adventure of fairy tales and nightmares come true, two very different hearts must work together to face unimaginable horrors.

Website: https://torilundell.com/
Buy Now on Amazon, Barnes&Noble & More

The Abandoned Crown Series
by Cerynn McCain

When Alice was captured her life ended.

Tortured and broken for thirteen years left her small and afraid. But when the guard assigned to her torture helped her escape, she was given a brief glimpse of hope.

Until she forgot.

Now hiding in a city full of its own secrets, Alice must work hard to remember why she came here.

Before it's too late.

Instagram: @cerynnmccain_author
Buy Now on Amazon

R.E.M.
by Ashley Schaller

Gwendolyn Gonzales would do anything for her best friend. Even allow herself to be dragged through Macy's dreams by a British coffeeholic who claims to be Macy's Dream Guardian. The rules of the Dream are simple: blend in and don't die. When Macy's dreams take a turn for the worst, following the rules may be harder than it seems. And may end in deadly consequences.

Instagram: @ashleyschallerauthor
Website: ashleyschaller.com
Buy Now on Amazon

ASHLEY SCHALLER